CAPE MAY

GHOST

STORIES

BOOK 2

.

by

CHARLES J. ADAMS III

EXETER HOUSE BOOKS

CAPE MAY GHOST STORIES, BOOK II

©Charles J. Adams III

Research Editor: David J. Seibold

For information, write to:
EXETER HOUSE BOOKS
P.O. Box 8134
Reading, Pennsylvania 19603

THIRD PRINTING 2001

PRINTED IN THE UNITED STATES OF AMERICA

B+T 8.95 10/02

ISBN   1-880683-11-3

TABLE OF CONTENTS

CAPE MAY GHOST STORIES · BOOK TWO

Introduction

Join us as we again explore the dark side of one of the most charming and alluring resort cities on the East Coast of the United States.

Cape May.

The name evokes thoughts of sun-drenched beaches, fun-filled summers, shady streets and sidewalks, and the pastel and gingerbread of the hundreds of Victorian shops, hotels, bed & breakfasts, and private homes.

Cape May.

There is a certain sense of dignity here. A certain sense of being—that much has passed before you came to see what you could see, do what you could do, and feel what you could feel in this almost magical place.

Cape May.

Pirates, poseurs, pioneers, politicians.

Inventors, investors, impostors.

Fires, floods, follies, fools...and phantoms.

All have come to call and have left their marks on this remarkable land where bay meets sea and cedars meet sand.

By day, Cape May bustles with activity. From the strand to the streets, people wander about in a never-ending search to get away from their mundane lives somewhere else.

By night, after the sun slithers beyond the bayside beach named for the eternal phenomenon, the "today" parts

CAPE MAY GHOST STORIES · BOOK TWO

of the city are bathed in bright illumination.

But in old Cape May–the *real* Cape May–lanterns cast their eerie glimmers through craggy branches. A cat squeals at the end of a darkened alley. Footsteps creak somewhere behind you.

Your eyes dart in the darkness. Your lips tighten, your skin bubbles, as something–*something*–skulks just beyond the dim glow of the next street light.

You want to run, to hide, to escape. You don't want to deal with the mysteries of the night.

And yet, you want to walk briskly and boldly into that night. You want to meet and deal with whatever that *something* may have been.

Was it a passing shadow cast by an unseen being crossing up ahead? Was it real, or just imagined?

Was it...was it...a *ghost?*

Do you really want to know?

Of course you do.

Come along, then, as we walk those seemingly sinister streets and enter some of the buildings from which that *something* may have emerged.

Perhaps we have ventured there before. More than a decade has passed since last we sought the spirits of town and country on this mysterious cape.

It's time we turned our collars up to shield the icy chills, gathered our senses, held hands, and ventured once again into the Cape May some folks are unaware–or afraid–of encountering.

Are you alone? Perhaps you should not be.

What was that muted sound you just heard? Was that

CAPE MAY GHOST STORIES · BOOK TWO

a dim, glowing figure that drifted past you, over there in the corner? Perhaps you should investigate.

Perhaps it can wait.

The Phantom Cabins

The time: Labor Day weekend, 1952. The place: On the way to Cape May.

The story: One you will find very hard to believe.

In the process of searching for ghost stories on New Jersey's storied southern cape, we were urged to contact one Al Goodman, who, someone said, had a most unusual tale to tell.

Indeed he did.

Al admitted that his story had all the earmarks of something from Alfred Hitchcock, but assured that he had not been influenced by the film maker in the incident which follows.

He does not now, nor never has, believed in ghosts, or that UFOs have transported aliens to Planet Earth.

Everything he said happened, happened. Just as you are about to read.

As the holiday weekend began, Al and a girlfriend headed "down the shore" from his home in the Strawberry Mansion section of Philadelphia.

They knew that along the pikes and highways, there would be plenty of roadside accommodations from which they could choose.

It was to be an idyllic Labor Day weekend for the two young people.

As Al and his friend wound their way south on Route 9, the light of day and the energy of the couple ebbed. They decided it was time to find a motel and retire for the night.

They stopped at the first place and were turned away. No vacancy.

They passed another, and then another motel. One after another, they flashed "No Vacancy" signs.

The highway commerce thinned as they drove deeper into the interior. They were beginning to panic.

There was little moonlight. The night was dark. The highway grew lonely and shrouded in a canopy of trees.

Al shielded his eyes from oncoming headlights when his own lights shone on something dead ahead.

Just off the right side of the roadway, there was a large—maybe five by ten feet—sign board. It read something like:

Black paint dripped from the crudely-scrawled lettering. The "E" was backwards, and the arrow pointed into what appeared to be the thick of the south Jersey pine forest.

Still, there was hope that this sign, perhaps a hasty replacement for a better one which had been blown down by a recent storm, or perhaps a temporary billboard for a new establishment, pointed the way to a quiet place with a soft bed.

The young man and young woman debated briefly as to whether they should follow that arrow into the pines and seek their haven of rest.

As they talked things over, Al slowed and noticed the narrow dirt road the arrow pointed toward.

They agreed they had nothing to lose by following the sign and seeing what they could see.

There was barely enough space for Al to wheel his wide car from the highway onto the dirt road.

Stones and shells crushed under the weight of his tires as Al drove ever so cautiously down the lane.

Branches scratched the sides of the car and leaves brushed against the windows. The wheels bore the brunt of several ruts and holes in the road, but Al persevered.

The road seemed to envelop the car. It was like driving into an ever-tightening funnel until at once there was a clearing.

Al pounded the brake pedal as he noticed a pair of rusted railroad tracks crossing just ahead. The rails sagged on rotted ties and weeds strangled the long-abandoned right of way.

The car *blub-blubbed* over the tracks and continued along the spooky roadway.

Again, Al's headlights beamed onto a most unexpected–and unsettling–sight.

A rickety old house, looking like any old and "haunted" house in any old movie loomed in the distance.

Al honked his horn to summon whoever might be inside the rundown place.

In this black-and-white world there emerged a bony, disheveled, old man. He was carrying not a flashlight, but a lantern.

The man was bent over. He squinted into the headlights and swung his lantern.

In a voice scratched by cigarettes and deepened by the years, he bellowed, "Who's there?"

Al looked around him and stepped slowly from the car. He explained that he and his, er, wife were looking for a place to stay for the night.

The old man cocked his head and raised his lantern to shine its dim glow on Al's female friend.

"Come with me," the old gent beckoned.

The couple followed him to a broken-down shed. In it was a metal frame bed which looked as it hadn't been slept in for decades.

Next to the bed was a dusty night stand and a dustier bowl.

This, they were told, was to be their haven of rest for the night, if they so chose.

Al's friend grew more nervous as they stood in the eerie "cabin." It should have been obvious to Al that she wanted nothing to do with the place.

Still, Al asked where the bathroom was located.

The old man pointed to an outhouse a few feet down a vine-tangled path.

Al was also quite ill at ease, and felt the bathroom situation was a good way out of an unnerving predicament.

He told the old man the accommodations wouldn't do. Obviously angered by that refusal, the old man offered to show them a room in the main house. There, he said with irritated sarcasm, they might find conditions more to their "citified" tastes.

Obligingly, Al and his friend followed the lantern man to the house.

Inside the front door, Al felt all sense of time draining away. He felt he had entered a warp and was walking into a lost age.

Dusty and musty, the old house seemed to close in around them. The old man led them through the parlor and up a narrow staircase to what was obviously the attic.

Halfway up, Al halted the journey. Needing an excuse to beat a hasty retreat from this odd place, he made up a cock-and-bull story that his, er, wife had bad feet and had to soak them every three hours.

It was a lousy, ludicrous story, he now admits, but one which facilitated their escape from the clutches of the weird.

The old man sneered as if he did not believe the bad feet tale, and he angrily told the couple to leave.

Al and his friend were more than ready to accommodate him. The scurried to the car, locked the doors behind them, and made their way back down the strange, dark lane.

Farther down the road, they found a more suitable place to stay, and there they spent their Labor Day weekend.

All day Saturday, however, they could do little else than ponder what happened to them the previous night.

They were almost preoccupied with the incident, the place, and that odd man.

So intrigued by it all, and so unwilling to accept that

the bizarre episode really ever took place (although then as now both affirm it did!), Al and his friend decided to retrace their steps and seek "Mae's Cabins" in the reassuring light of day.

They drove to the precise spot the sign was located. Al was careful on Friday night to remember certain landmarks, in case anything untoward might have happened.

Just as he drove to what he had believed was the location of the sign and the road to the dilapidated old house, there was nothing. No sign, no road.

Al pulled into a nearby service station and inquired about "Mae's." The attendant there, and in other stations in the vicinity, never heard of the place.

It was as if that sign, that road, that old house, and that cranky old man never, ever existed.

As if all of it emerged like Brigadoon from the mist of a Cape May night.

To this day, Al Goodman swears the story is true and unembellished.

The retired engineer and World War II veteran now lives in a small town in South Jersey, and among his many life stories is this most peculiar and perplexing mystery.

All that we see or seem
Is but a dream within a dream.
    ...Edgar Allan Poe, 1827

CAPE MAY GHOST STORIES · BOOK TWO

Forever an Angel

It is one of the most spectacular and respected bed & breakfast inns in the United States.

It has been featured on television programs and in magazines across the world.

It is a glittering, Grand Victorian gem which exemplifies the splendor that is Cape May.

It is the Angel of the Sea.

It is haunted.

As the Angel of the Sea is not your typical B&B, the spirit which rambles through its elegant chambers is not an ordinary ghost.

It is, according to a woman who preferred to be called only "Bridget" and referred to only as the "Cruise Director," what the Angel of the Sea folks tend to call their "angel."

The building—make that *buildings* —of the Angel are stories unto themselves. Daily tours of the grounds detail the incredible architectural appurtenances and restoration triumphs involved in breathing life back into the National Historic Landmark structures.

Philadelphia chemist William Weightman built his seashore mansion in the center of Cape May city in 1850. Thirty years later, the fabulously wealthy man decided that civilization had closed in on him too tightly and had his sprawling home moved to Ocean Street and Beach Drive, where it would provide him with a sweeping view of the sea.

The big house was battered by the Nor'easter of 1963, and was again moved north to its present location at Trenton Street and Beach Drive.

During the 1980s, the buildings served as dormitory housing for employees of the nearby Christian Admiral Hotel, Congress Hall, and Shelton College.

Through most of that decade, the old Weightman mansion steadily deteriorated until municipal officials said it was uninhabitable.

John and Barbara Girton purchased the place in 1988, and with labor and love, the builder and his wife rode herd over a massive, $3.5 million restoration project.

In 1990, the Angel of the Sea opened as the largest B&B in Cape May and one of the most historically-significant restorations in the country.

It was during the period of the building's decline, in about 1969, when tragedy struck the declining boarding house.

A late-teenage girl who was employed at the Christian Admiral returned to her room at what is now the Angel of the Sea, only to find herself without her keys.

The girl was in a hurry. Her shift at the big hotel was done, and she was headed for church. She had precious little time to shower and change.

She could have hurried back to the Christian Admiral to retrieve her key, but something she noticed in the corridor of her dormitory floor led her to another decision.

She noticed the ease with which a window at the end of the hallway could be opened, and reasoned that with

The ghost of a teenage girl is said to haunt the stately Angel of the Sea.

relatively little effort, she could crawl out that window, shinny along a ledge to her room, open her own window, and crawl into her room.

It was the worst of all decisions.

She opened the first window and clambered onto the ledge. She found her room window, but also found that the screen on it was a rather tight fit.

It took a little effort to pry the screen from the frame, and as she applied that effort, the screen sprung out suddenly, smacked her in the forehead, and sent her tumbling to her death.

Some time later, a groundskeeper found the girl's broken body between the two buildings of what is now the Angel of the Sea.

To this day, those who know will not reveal the exact location of the ledge, the window, the room, or the spot the girl's body was found.

"I've learned my lesson," Bridget said, avowing that she would not disclose those details because guests might be uncomfortable knowing they are staying in a room where such an untimely death occurred.

And yet, Bridget was not the least hesitant to confirm that over the years the spirit of the teenager has made itself known in the big inn.

Apparently as mischievous in the afterlife as she was while among the mortals, the girl's ghost has provided some disconcerting experiences for both guests and employees of the Angel of the Sea.

The spirit seems to have an affinity for electronic and electrical devices.

It is not unusual for lamps to light or be extinguished by the roving energy of the unfortunate lass.

Bridget mused that the youthful wraith apparently likes to watch television, as TV sets have been known to turn on "by themselves" from time to time.

Guests and housekeepers have noticed items moving mysteriously, disappearing from one spot and reappearing in another, and falling from tables and dressers.

And, furniture not designed to rock and sway has been felt rocking and swaying—in motion attributed to the "angel."

Most fittingly, given the circumstances of the teenager's demise, her spirit has been said to lock and unlock doors in certain parts of the inn.

Had she, in life, been able to unlock one certain door, she might still be alive.

While Bridget could not be coerced to give the number of the affected room, she did say the incident took place on the third floor in the inn's "second building," the one toward New Jersey Street.

There have been no known sightings of the spirit, although Bridget quipped, "We once had a cognac-induced sighting" few agreed was valid.

Still, those who hold the legends and lore of the classic inn dear truly believe that within its walls glides the sorrowful and gentle angel of the Angel.

what beck'ning ghost along the moonlight shade
Invites my steps, and points to yonder glade?
...Alexander Pope, 1717

CAPE MAY GHOST STORIES · BOOK TWO

From cupola to street level, Spiaggi is the site of several hauntings.

15

Gloria

By the time you read this, what was the highly-respected "New International" cuisine "Restaurant Maureen" will have made a transition to a decidedly Italian restaurant called "Spiaggi."

Same location.

Same owners.

Same chef.

Same ghost.

It is regarded as the oldest establishment in Cape May to hold and use its liquor license, and the 150-seat ocean front dining room on the second floor Beach and Decatur is one of the most praised restaurants in the city.

Built in 1879, the four-story Victorian building is topped with a cupola, and it is in that top level and other upper floors where strange incidents have caught employees off-guard for several years.

The restaurants on the site have gone by the names of "Denizot's Ocean View House," "Henri's," "Arnold's," "Summer," and "Gloria's."

It is from that last reference where the spirit of Spiaggi received its name.

"Different things have happened here," said Megan

Wojnar, a hostess at Katie O'Brien's, a tavern/restaurant on the first floor of the building at the time of this writing.

"Up in the cupola," she continued, "many folks say they can feel her presence."

More than just a feeling, this ghost they call Gloria may have actually left a photographic imprint.

Ms. Wojnar, a South Philadelphian interviewed while she was working during the summer at Katie O'Brien's, has heard all the stories.

"They say it was a baby, and supposedly she was either killed somehow or died a crib death. I was told it happened on the third or fourth floor. She even appears once in a while, I'm told. A lot of people say they can feel her, though."

Mounted on a wall near the entrance to the downstairs lounge is a misty, black-and-white photograph. It is believed to date from about 1900, as the name "Summers" is visible on it. At the turn of that century, the establishment was known as "Summers."

More curiously, however, the photograph reveals the haunting form of a baby which seems to be trapped within a column of the old eatery. The position of the child makes any investigator hard-pressed to explain just how it appears where it does.

"You can see that there's no way that a baby could be standing anywhere near there," Megan Wojnar said as she pointed out the eerie image.

Could this be the ghost of the house?

Maureen and Stephen Horn bought the property in 1982 and are responsible for its stunning restoration.

Maureen secured the photograph when she and her husband bought the place.

"I had the picture sepiatoned and enlarged," she recalled. "And when you look in the photograph, you look in the column of the post in the bar. The photograph has a baby in that column. But if you look closely, if you think it was a mirror, you would see that there was no way a baby could be in that position."

Shortly after the Horns bought the building, previous owners and tenants spoke freely about the ghost.

"It's a wonderful place," Maureen noted. "When you stand in an upper floor during a strong wind, the building sways and you feel the cold breezes. There's nothing ghostly about that, it's just because it's a wooden building."

Stephen G. Horn, bartender, cook, and son, does not shrug at the notion of the ghost they call Gloria.

"Ever since I've been little, weird things have happened here, especially upstairs," he said.

"A lot of times I'd go upstairs and I would hear somebody moving around. The hair on the back of my neck would stand up," he added.

One independent psychic has confirmed a presence in the building. It is felt to be young, female, and extremely docile.

It could, the psychic who wished to remain nameless said, become more active during and after any renovations which might have taken place in the transition from Maureen's to Spiaggi.

Why that transition? Maureen said of her husband, who studied in Italy, "He's going through a midlife culinary crisis."

Hopefully, Gloria the ghost will understand that...and appreciate Italian food!

Look closely—is that the ghostly image of a baby in this old photograph of the restaurant at Beach and Decatur?

A ghost looking for a good time haunts the Southern Mansion.

Party On...and on...and on

The meticulous conversion of one of Cape May's grand old buildings was just getting underway when we aimed our inquiring minds on what is now called "The Southern Mansion."

The sprawling estate once belonged to the fabulously-wealthy Philadelphian George Allen, but at press time was establishing itself as what spokeswoman Barbara Wilde unashamedly called, "the fanciest, nicest place in town!"

No doubt, The Southern Mansion, with its mirrored, brilliantly-lit, 400-to-500 square feet rooms, seemingly endless veranda, ornate Italianate styling and luxurious appointments will be a fine–in Ms. Wilde's words– "Boutique Hotel."

But we were there not for the estate's architectural integrity. We wanted to hear the ghost stories about the place.

Built in 1863, the 720 Washington Street mansion and lawns sprawl across two acres and is indeed one of the most remarkable structures in Cape May.

The Wilde family purchased the property in 1996, and according to one noted psychic, they are in store for some supernatural surprises once their renovations are completed.

More on that later.

"Oh, yes," said Ms. Wilde, "we have had people reporting that they have seen a well-dressed woman in ghostly form here. But most of all, it's the perfume."

Yes, should you tour or stay in The Southern Mansion, be prepared for the pleasant waft of perfume to tickle your nose.

"It's a good presence," Ms. Wilde continued. "It's not scary or anything.

"Since we've been here, a lot of people have come up and asked if we have any ghosts here. Then, we have had people really telling us that they smell an expensive perfume in places they'd least expect. I thought they were crazy," she said.

Capt. George Allen built the mansion, and it eventually fell into the hands of a niece named Esther.

"The ghost," Ms. Wilde said, "is probably Esther. And, let me say that she appears to be quite the party girl.

"People have said they have seen a woman looking at them. They have felt her presence, have heard her laughing, have seen her dancing. And there's always the perfume. They say it's a very expensive kind of perfume," she noted.

One of the most recognizable and striking signs Esther may be present is the unmistakable sound of the rustling of an old-fashioned petticoat drifting down a corridor or across a room.

Barbara Wilde has grown to love the old mansion, and has come to accept any presence that may inhabit it.

"The only thing I have experienced," she said, "is that there is something here, for certain, and it is definitely feminine. That's all I can tell you. It's definitely female."

But, she added that there is one hot spot in the old Allen home.

"There's one room with two small windows and one

larger window. There is most definitely a different kind of feeling in there.

"I heard that someone died in that room. And I felt what I felt in there before I found that out. It's not a horrible 'they're-gonna-get-you' kind of feeling. It's just a different feeling from the rest of the house. You go in there and there's a nice, comfortable feeling in there."

A paranormal researcher did visit and "read" The Southern Mansion and did sense "Esther," the "party ghost." And, she took the "party ghost" to its logical extension and actually determined that in one particular room there seems to be erotic, illicit, and eternal affairs being carried out. Ethereal affairs of both the heart...and the body.

That same psychic sensed great levels of tension in the spiritual energies inside the mansion. She speculated that George Allen may have had a big financial falling-out and both departed this world with much unfinished business between them.

Their spirits—along with Esther's and whomever is doing whatever to whomever in that one particular room—are very strong, but quite benign.

When the researcher wandered the halls and rooms of The Southern Mansion in early summer, 1996, she did predict that in the year which followed that reading, the ghosts of the old Allen mansion would make themselves well known.

Simply stated, The Southern Mansion, according to that one paranormal investigator, has within it the strongest energy of any building in Cape May.

The Doctor's Inn is a charming—and haunted—location in the heart of Cape May Court House.

The Doctor's Ghost

We leave the streets of Cape May for this story and venture into the busy confines of the county seat, aptly named Cape May Court House.

It is a town where commercial and governmental activity mingle at a rapid pace, a geographic and cultural crossroads of Cape May County.

And in at least one pocket of serenity in the town, there is a very beautiful, a very historic, and some say a very haunted place.

The recorded history of that place can be traced as far back as 1690, when a colonial physician was granted 1,000 acres by the king of England.

A parcel of that grant was transferred by that doctor to Shamgar Hand, one of the founding fathers of Cape May County.

For nearly two centuries, the land was owned by a succession of Hand family members until Danielia Hand married Dr. John Wiley and the couple decided to build a comfortable home at what is now 2 North Main Street in Cape May C.H.

The core of the building which stands there today was constructed in 1854. A few years after Dr. and Mrs. Wiley settled in their new home, duty called and the good doctor was pressed into service for the Union Army in the Civil War.

CAPE MAY GHOST STORIES · BOOK TWO

It must be remembered that Cape May County is well south of a protracted Mason-Dixon Line, and while there were certain mixed loyalties during what deep southerners called the "War of Northern Aggression," New Jersey was a "northern" state.

Dr. Wiley felt great compassion for the plight of southern slaves, and it is generally accepted that his property was a "safe house" along the route of the "Underground Railroad."

When the present owner of the house was excavating for the construction of an addition, workers discovered the sealed opening of a tunnel which once spirited runaway slaves from the stable to the kitchen.

For many decades after the Wileys last lived in the house, it fell into steady decline until it was abandoned in the 1980s.

At that point, authorities recognized the importance of the property to county and regional history, and attempted to find a salvor who would restore the house and land to its past glory.

Enter: Carolyn Crawford, M.D..

The neonatologist fell in love with the place, jumped through the regulatory hoops of the Resolution Trust Co. (the old house was a victim of the savings and loan crisis of the early 1990s), and set out to save the old doctor's house.

Enter: The Doctor's Inn at King's Grant.

Dr. Crawford wrote the prescription for restoration, as she did at the Colonnade Inn, over in Sea Isle City. She and a team of dedicated designers, decorators, and contractors did more than anyone might have expected and created a

European-style country inn, fine dining restaurant, and island of Old World tranquility within a sea of hustle and bustle.

Deciding what to call the inn provided little challenge. Built by a doctor, continued as doctors' offices for many years, and now restored by a doctor, the house built upon a king's grant was accorded a noble name.

The inn has drawn the attention of leading B&B and restaurant reviewers, and has a certain character which befits its history.

And, as you may have guessed, part of that character involves a ghost.

Dr. Crawford said she is well aware that spirit energy can, and likely does, exist.

She lived in a house in Merion Station, Pa., which was said to be haunted, and had little problem believing or coping with the occasional time that wraith made itself known.

Now, the good doctor lives in The Doctor's Inn, and while she has not (yet) witnessed the ghost there, she remains open-minded that it is there, and respects the expressions of other reliable folks who have told her of their encounters with the supernatural.

"I have been told, although I haven't experienced the presence myself, that there is a little girl who runs through the house, closing some doors and opening others," she said.

"She's a very happy little girl, they say, about eight or nine years old. She has long hair, a long dress, and has a big bow in the back of her hair.

"Several people have said they have felt her presence," she continued.

The spirit of a long-haired little girl is said to wander through the Doctor's Inn.

Those who claim to have felt or seen the youthful ghost include several employees, guests, and a trusted chef who, Dr. Crawford said, was "quite convinced" that the three-story main house is, in the vernacular, "haunted."

The ghost is harmless, but can be a bit feisty at times.

"Downstairs and on the first floor in particular," Dr. Crawford reported, "is where the doors and cabinets have opened and closed, seemingly on their own."

Better still, though, there have been certain people who have spent time on that first floor–in Dr. Wiley's old examining room, where his photographic portrait hangs in tribute–who have, in Dr. Crawford's words, "caught fleeting glances of the little girl."

Dr. Crawford has no problem accepting, and perhaps at some time even welcoming, her elusive house guest.

She recognizes, along with many others who have lovingly restored historic old houses, that a ghost–especially an innocent and only slightly mischievous ghost such as that in The Doctor's Inn–adds a certain "character" to a place.

Vex not his ghost: O! let him pass! he hates him
That would upon the rack of this tough world
Stretch him out longer.

...William Shakespeare

29

The Shepherd in the Night

[A letter received following publication of Cape May Ghost Stories (Book One)]

I have just completed your book. I enjoyed it. I also noticed that you are continuing your quest to research and record any and all stories of the supernatural from Cape May County.

I vacationed in Wildwood every summer since I was an infant until the age of 22.

I've always had a special relationship with the town itself. To me, it's more than just a town, it's a living entity. Probably sounds a little strange. At any rate, I've lived in various other states, but I always seem to move back here.

Odd things seem to be a way of life with me. The main one that took place here in Wildwood may be of interest to you.

When I was 28 years old, my husband and I were living on 15th Ave. in Wildwood. One evening during the summer I decided to take a walk on the boardwalk and ended up going to a movie.

The movie let out a little after 9 p.m. and I started walking home through town.

The main strip was all brightly lit up with neon lights and lots of people.

Gradually, however, I ventured into a residential area where it was all very dark and I do not remember any street lights at all.

I became aware that I had a long walk home and grew frightened–not about anything supernatural–frightened of the real world and what could happen to a young woman out at night alone.

I remember saying a quick prayer that God would allow me a safe trip back home.

When I finished, I turned my head to the right and peered into a very dark side street.

Out of the darkness emerged an immense dog–casually, yet with stately air, coming toward me.

I am a dog lover and so I had no fear of this beautiful animal. He walked right up to me and sat in front of me looking at me.

I remember saying "hello there, are you going to escort me home?"

I petted his head and told him no one would bother me with him around. He was a German Shepherd, mostly black with a moderate amount of tan.

Like clockwork, he moved when I moved. He stayed with me with no coaxing on my part.

I chatted to him all the way home. He came into my home and slept by me (he was on the floor).

I told my husband what a godsend the dog had been.

The next morning I woke up to find the shepherd sitting up, looking at me.

When he had my attention he turned and walked to the door and waited for me to let him out.

I did.

I watched him leave the house, but I never really saw him *go*.

It seemed he was just not there anymore.

Many years later I bought two German Shepherds and learned how shepherds do not take to strange and unknown people. They are family dogs.

This makes the behavior of that shepherd on that dark night in Wildwood that much more bizarre.

Sincerely,

Rebecca N. Witbeck

The Ghosts of the Hoffman House

Thursday, August 17, 1871: Along what is now Bayshore Road, 35-year old Jonathan Hoffman and his wife were returning to their home after a pleasant visit with the neighboring Parsons family.

The Hoffmans, who had for three years lived in the white frame house and worked a large garden around it, were crossing the road onto their property.

As they approached a low fence and a natural hedge of elderberry bushes, a gunshot rattled the quiet of the early evening.

Mrs. Hoffman shrieked as a bullet ripped into her husband's side. He fell into a bloody pool and was dead in mere moments.

"Mrs. Hoffman ran back to the Parsons' pale an trembling with fear to tell what had occurred," wrote a *Cape May Ocean Wave* reporter who covered the story, "and soon the alarm was spread from one to another until all the neighbors were aroused. But the murderer succeeded in getting away."

The newspaper called it "the most shocking, cold-blooded murder ever perpetrated in this locality."

Upon investigation, it was discovered that the killer was apparently one of a band of thieves who were ransacking the Hoffman house while the couple was away.

That investigation in what was a fairly remote part of Cape May County at the time, was criticized by the writer.

"After the fatal deed had been committed," it was written, "there was no extended effort on the part of those about to find the assassin. Indeed, information was not brought to the authorities until the following morning.

"If the underbrush, or woods, from which the shot was fired had been promptly scoured by a body of

determined armed men, the murderer could not have easily escaped, and it is somewhat surprising that some such effort was not made."

No matter, Jonathan Hoffman was dead. The morning after the killing, the victim—described as a hard-working, religious man—was back in his home, "cold and stiff in death."

The murder infuriated residents of the cape. The mayor of Cape May City offered a $500 reward for the apprehension of the killer, and Justice of the Peace Lemuel Leaming conducted an inquest which brought together the leading citizens of the time and place. Total cost for the inquest, incidentally: $17.05.

The Hoffman murder, an 1873 gun attack on a county Freeholder, and the escape of five prisoners from the crude Cape May County jail caused citizens to reassess their "quiet" part of New Jersey and address the region's law enforcement system.

Further details of the shooting and its aftermath are for the historians. Let us now flip the pages of time ahead more than 125 years and focus on the ghostly goings-on in the old Hoffman house.

And considering what happened in and around that house way back when, those goings-on may surprise you.

"We have three ghosts here," said Pat Calfina, who now resides in the house.

"I've never heard of anyone who had a cat's ghost [Editor's note: We have!], but it's real distinct. On the second floor you can feel the cat walking on the bed," she continued.

"I have a real aversion about animals sleeping in the same room as me," she added. "I always keep my bedroom door closed when I am in bed."

"But I feel the very distinct foot steps of a cat walking across the bed on the second floor. I would reach out to grab the cat and find nothing.

"Then, I would get up to remove the cat. The doors were still closed, and there was no cat in the room. When I would go downstairs to check, our family cat would be fast asleep on the couch or chair," she noted. "Anyone who has slept on the second floor has felt the cat walk across that bed."

Pat's daughter, Terri, confirmed her mother's observations. She pointed out that the pawfalls of the invisible feline actually make imprints and create waves on an upstairs waterbed.

While the cat's ghost remains elusive and unexplainable, the two other spirits of the Hoffman house have created more anxiety among those who have experienced them.

"My daughter was decorating for one of the children's parties," Pat Calfina said. "She was up on a chair, hanging streamers from the ceiling. The children had been taken out, to get them from under foot. My daughter and I were alone in the house. I said to her, 'I really like childrens' parties.'

"This faint, little voice from out of nowhere replied very plainly, 'so do I.' The two of us were still alone in the dining room.

"We both went, *ooh!* It was definitely a little boy. We've never been able to find out who the little boy is, but he's here, somewhere."

Several months later, Pat was preparing for a baby shower in the kitchen, setting out a buffet table of pastries. "I bent down to get napkins out of a cabinet when I was hit in the back of the head with a pastry. I thought, OK, I don't know how that fell off the counter and hit me, but it did. So I threw the pastry away and bent down again. I was hit by a second pastry! I stood up and looked around the room. I was alone. I said in a firm voice, 'OK, these cakes were expensive, so we should not be playing with them! Knock it off!

"I had no more problems."

Terri described the lad as wearing dark pants, no shoes, and a white shirt. He has an affinity, she claimed, for toys—especially Power Rangers, the rage of the 1990s.

"He plays with my daughter all the time," she said, "but she doesn't like to talk about it.

"When she heard you were coming here today to talk about our ghosts, she said 'we're not going in my room!'"

While some may dismiss these entities as figments of the imagination, it is more difficult to discount the energy of a third presence Pat Calfina said inhabits her home.

"We call her Mrs. Gandy," she said.

According to Pat, a Mrs. Gandy was the last of the Hoffman family to reside in the house, and before she passed on, she sold the property out of the family for the first time since it was built at the time of the Civil War.

The woman is remembered as a gentle sort who was childless, but was kind to all children in the area. Pat was told Mrs. Gandy would often bake goodies and distribute them to young folks who lived nearby.

Appropriately, Pat said the woman's spirit is quite attached to her granddaughter.

In fact, there was one incident when the subconscious "appearance" of Mrs. Gandy may have helped save the little girl.

Pat told of a time not too long ago when her granddaughter was on the back patio playing by herself. Pat was inside the house and felt Mrs. Gandy's presence. Pat believed the spirit was urging her to hasten to the little girl's side.

Pat rushed to the patio to find that her granddaughter had swallowed a small toy and was choking. She removed the obstruction and comforted the little girl.

Terri claimed to have seen Mrs. Gandy dressed in a nightgown, gliding across the floor. "You don't actually see her," Pat countered. "It's more like a movement out of the corner of your eye. You're just aware that she's there."

Pat's husband, Phil, has also had experiences with the resident wraiths.

Describing his encounters with Mrs. Gandy, he said, "You'll be standing there and she'll just walk by. She walks slowly, and she's gone.

"I don't think she's a vicious or harmful person, I think she's just lost and confused."

Pat agreed. As for the little boy, she tends to believe he's more a protector and playmate for her granddaughter.

And for Mrs. Gandy? "I think she's still here because she's very upset that she was the one to sell the property out of the family line."

AN INDIAN GHOST AT COLD SPRING VILLAGE?

Phil Calfina, who does contract work at Cold Spring Village, near the Hoffman house, told of the ghost of an Indian he said he encountered at the popular tourist attraction.

"I've had incidents there where I'd be sitting on a bench, I'd see someone, say something to them, and I'd turn around and they'd be gone.

"And one time, I met an Indian there, around dusk. I was putting leaves over where the actual Cold Spring is, and I saw him walking down the nature trail there in the secluded area.

"He walked by, acknowledged me, and I started to say something to him, but as I did, he shook his head, and disappeared into the sunset!"

Calfina knows that there are often costumed characters who stroll the village. "This," he affirmed, "was not one of them. This was something I'll never be able to explain."

Things That Go Bump...Explained?

In their handsome promotional brochure, Jim and Rosalie Kelly inform prospective guests that they will be "greeted at the door with a warm hello and invited to unwind." Guests at Kelly's Celtic Inn "will sense the slower pace, elegant surroundings and vacation mood of the Inn; much as it was in the 1880s."

They most certainly will. It was that sense of ambience, evident even on the exterior of the 24 Ocean Street property, that drew the chroniclers of the supernatural to the Celtic Inn.

The place seemed to have character. And often with character comes a ghost story or two.

There *are* ghost stories in the Celtic Inn, and Rosalie Kelly was cordial enough to share them. But, she was also practical enough to all but nullify them by offering explanations.

Rosalie told the tale in a measured conversational gait.

"In our third floor rear room," she said, "guests have commented on two specific incidents that happened repeatedly.

"One was that a rocking chair would move, and the explanation I can give for that is that there is an old jalousie door out to the third floor deck. When we would put the Plexiglas panel in the door in the winter, it didn't fit properly.

So, the wind would come through the panel and move the rocking chair. We've since replaced the door, and the 'ghost' is gone."

Mayhaps, Rosalie, mayhaps.

The second incident involves a phenomenon that provided enough chills for a party of guests that one of them recorded it in the guest ledger.

It took place in the same room of the inn, which was built in the early 1880s as the summer home of a Philadelphia baker.

From the deck of that third floor room, guests are accorded a sweeping view of the ocean. And at least one visitor was accorded something even more exciting.

The date was October 29, 1994. The author shall remain nameless:

Today is S___'s wedding. All of the bridesmaids spent S____'s last night as a single woman on the top floor here.

S_____ and I stayed in this room while other bridesmaids stayed in two other rooms.

Strange goings on in those rooms! About midnight, their beds started shaking. They all ran screaming into our room. They wound up being locked out of their rooms and ended up sleeping scared to death in our room.

What excitement! This is a night we'll never forget! We loved it!

With a grinning wink and an arched-eyebrow tsk-tsk-tsk, Rosalie Kelly dismissed the entry and the experience as group hysteria—and an architectural glitch.

The "shaking bed" had been reported before. It

seemed that the afflicted third floor room was uncarpeted at the time, and as there was no sub-floor, a five-speed, large ceiling fan was attached to the joist.

When the fan turned, the bed vibrated. When the fan was replaced and the upstairs room was carpeted, that "ghost," too, was "exorcised."

Such is life in the quest for ghost stories. Kelly's Celtic Inn still has character, but whether it is of the good, old-fashioned, ghostly kind, that remains to be seen.

CONGRESS HALL QUIRKS

Joe Seddon, who doubled as a member of the maintenance crew and tour guide at the magnificent Congress Hall in Cape May, shared his story about the landmark building.

"There's a specific room here in the hotel that I've been in. At the end of the tours, I go through and I shut out all the lights.

"Throughout the course of a day, I'll go up and there's that one room where the door is always open and the lights are shut out.

"I know, because we don't turn off the lights until the end of the night and this door is extremely hard to open.

"This has happened as many as six times in one day when I have gone up and that door is wide open.

"On the third floor," Seddon continued, "there's a room in which one light always stays lit. I'll go up there and make a point to shut the lights off again, and the light is back on."

Seddon stopped short of blaming these glitches on anything supernatural, but admitted that there seems to be no logical explanation for many of the strange events.

"The way this building creaks," Seddon said, "it seems as if it's moaning. It seems as if the building itself is alive!"

A kindly spirit named Esmerelda guards the Inn at 22 Jackson.

Esmerelda

Little did we know that as we were researching the spirits in the Wicker Room of the Windward House at 24 Jackson Street, there was a ghost on the prowl just next door.

The Windward House ghost story is detailed in *Cape May Ghost Stories, Book One,* and it stands as one of the most interesting of all in any of the B&Bs in the historic center of town.

One property east of the Windward House is another bed & breakfast with a name which leaves no doubt as to its address: The Inn at 22 Jackson.

Its history is not unlike those of any number of Victorian inns in Cape May. Built as a summer home in 1899, the Inn was bought and restored by Barbara Carmichael and Chip Masemore.

Bedecked in pastel paints and gingerbread woodwork, the main house has five suites and an adjacent cottage provides total escape.

As Chip says, the Inn is "only a nine-iron shot from the beach."

The innkeepers have filled the place with antiques and novelties which is best described as "eclectic." Carmichael and Masemore have a collective sense of class touched with a sense of whimsy and humor.

Their inn has won rave reviews from guests and has picked up a Cape May Chamber of Commerce Beautification Award.

And, their inn has received notoriety because of the presence of one of its most enduring guests—Esmerelda.

First, let us not confuse Esmerelda with Minerva.

While neither is flesh and blood, Minerva is far more visible than Esmerelda.

All one has to do is wander into the parlor to pay a visit to dear Minerva. Unabashedly "bawdy" and quite the gadabout, Minerva is, according to Barbara Carmichael, the "head of housekeeping" at the Inn.

"She watches over our guests," said Ms. Carmichael, and is very prissy. Ocassionally, guests will bring her presents and share a spot of tea or a glass of spirits with her."

A gaily-dressed dowager, Minerva can always be counted on for some companionship. But do not, not ever, confuse her with her housemate named Esmerelda.

"Some guests do think Minerva is Esmerelda," Ms. Carmichael said. "And when that happens, Minerva gets quite haughty!"

Where the good-natured fun of Minerva ends, the supernatural mysteries of Esmerelda begin.

Esmerelda, you see, is not a costumed mannequin mascot.

Esmerelda is a ghost.

"She has been here for at least 50 years," Ms. Carmichael pointed out. "The stories of her go back to at least the late 1940s and early 1950s."

"I don't know how they started, but I do know that when Chip and I were bidding on the house and during the construction we were told about Esmerelda over and over.

"Some people who stayed here as children in the fifties talked about her.

"It was always good things. Esmerelda is very friendly and she particularly likes children. She really likes to play games, too."

One Esmerelda story remains without a final chapter. Perhaps a reader of this book will write it for the keepers of the Inn at 22 Jackson.

"There's a story that one lady who came to visit had come here a lot in the mid-1950s. She said that she and her sister were up in our turret, had an experience with Esmerelda, and made up a song about her to the tune of "The Ballad of Davy Crockett."

Who those guests were, and how those lyrics read, are still answers Carmichael and Masemore seek.

The innkeepers are quite comfortable sharing their stately old mansion with the ethereal Esmerelda. In fact, they have unofficially named a room after her.

The "Esmerelda Room," where some say the most ghostly activity has taken place, is actually one of two bedrooms in the suite formally called The Turret.

Interestingly, the building has, wrapped around its very top roof, a "widow's walk." The distinctive railing is so called because of the legend that the wives of men who have gone to sea would keep vigil for their husbands from that uppermost lookout post.

Too often in the treacherous days of sail, those

women who walked those rooftops would be rendered widows by the cruel sea.

In addition to that dour architectural curiosity, 22 Jackson St. also has that turret—sometimes called a "witch's hat" due to its pointed shape and ominous appearance.

Within that "witch's hat" are the rooms of the suite, and the Esmerelda Room.

Tranquil blue walls wrap around a king-sized bed, and doors open to a private deck with a glimpse of the Atlantic just beyond the rooftops of town. It is everything a Victorian Cape May B&B room can be.

And, it is haunted.

Barbara Carmichael continued talking about her invisible, and apparently permanent, guest. "Chip and I have not had any experiences of our own. But we cannot discount Esmerelda. Maybe we're just not child-like enough to be able to sense all of it.

"I will say that we have heard a lot about it.

"We even had a couple of guests who consider themselves intuitive and it's been amazing to us that without even being familiar with the house or the stories about Esmerelda, they have gone to that one room and other spots in the house and have detected her spirit."

The most chilling chain of events involving Esmerelda took place well after the traditional summer season of 1987.

Then, 22 Jackson St. was the address of an inn called the Cape Colony. Its owners were Eileen and Harry Angus.

Their story was detailed in the October, 1989, issue of *Philadelphia* magazine by writer Mike Mallowe.

Neither Harry nor Eileen were particularly interested

in, knowledgeable about, or very much concerned with ghosts.

They were merely a couple balancing newfound family life with the often overwhelming responsibilities of running a bed & breakfast inn.

There was always much to be done. Painting, repairing, cleaning, tending to guests. Those who own B&Bs know it is a full-time job. It is a lifestyle.

Eileen Angus was hard at work in her inn when there was a rapping at the front door.

She put down her labors for a spell and took a peek out a front window to see who was calling.

He was described as a tall, well-dressed, and dignified elderly man.

Appearing quite harmless and even gentle, the visitor smiled as Eileen opened the door.

The gent offered to shake her hand, and Eileen accepted after wiping the residue of her toils on her apron. He asked if she was the new owner.

Answering in the affirmative, Eileen felt somehow comfortable with the stranger. As it turned out, he had much to say about the old mansion the young couple was lovingly restoring.

His family once owned the building, he told her. He and his brothers were the painters and fixer-uppers of the family, and were very familiar with the idiosyncrasies of the old place.

As Eileen and the old man stood at the front door, and after he told her of his fondness for the house and the memories it held for him, an icy chill cut through Eileen's body.

The blast of frigid wind came as if from nowhere and slashed across her skin. Not a word was spoken for a few seconds, until the wind ceased and the temperature climbed.

Both distracted, Eileen and the old man blinked from their stares. Eileen fumbled for something to say, but the old man spoke first.

"Have you met Esmerelda?" he asked.

Eileen drew a deep breath and regained her composure. She asked if this "Esmerelda" was a relative of the old man's or a former owner.

No, the man said, Esmerelda lived up in the turret. Esmerelda died in the turret.

Esmerelda's ghost now *haunts* the turret, he told her.

Eileen was dumbfounded. A ghost? In her precious B&B? She demanded to know more.

The old stranger comforted her.

"She's quite dead," he said. "Quite harmless."

Esmerelda, he told Eileen, was a kindly woman, and would do no harm. But, he added, anyone who resides in the old house should be prepared to share the place with her spirit.

Eileen was riveted to his every word. Her eyes darted only when his eyes looked just over her shoulder and into the empty parlor.

The icy wind. The old man's piercing and wandering eyes. The ghost. Eileen was breathless.

So breathless was she that as the mystery man bade her farewell, she nodded mechanically and managed a weak smile. And, she never asked, nor was volunteered, his name.

As unexpectedly and almost mystically as the stranger with no name came into Eileen's life, he left.

For such a brief time there, the old man left a legacy which would literally haunt Eileen—and 22 Jackson Street, forever.

As it turned out, Eileen was familiar with the first volume of these Cape May ghost stories. She had read it, had a reasonable understanding of it, and was familiar with the feminine spirit in the place next door.

Now, she was informed by the anonymous visitor, she, too, shared her space with a spook!

Eileen tried to wash the notion from her mind. But, it lingered and teased and tossed about in her consciousness as she continued to renovate, repair, and restore the beautiful property.

The Pink Room! Aha! It was the Pink Room—a crusty, dusty, abandoned chamber up in the turret—which was Esmerelda's chamber in life and in death. And, she wondered, in *afterlife*, as well?

She was at first reluctant to have anything to do with what she called the Pink Room. But it had to, as every other room had to, be cleaned and outfitted for guests.

After it was, the guests came. In fact, one woman took the Pink Room for an entire season. Eileen hoped Esmerelda would be kind to her.

But it was from left field—or more properly, the first floor of the B&B—where a most unanticipated blow to Eileen's psyche came one quiet Cape May evening.

The large suite on the first floor had been let to a

family. After a day on the beach or boardwalk, or wherever, the family settled in for the night. Eileen's hectic day was beginning to smooth out when the mother of the family on the first floor sauntered up to her and asked for a few moments of her time.

In those moments, the mother stumbled and bumbled, but eventually was able to inquire if, by any chance, in any way, there was a ghost in the Cape Colony.

Eileen gulped. The mother gulped.

Eileen feigned ignorance of anything of the ghostly variety at her B&B, but listened intently as her guest told all.

It was a female ghost which appeared in the room. Mother and daughter both sensed it. Daughter felt the spirit sitting at the foot of her bed. Mother actually saw it.

The ghost appeared to the guest as a fleeting glimmer of movement in the corner of her eye. Nothing much more.

Still, the two women who were staying at the Cape Colony felt no fear, more a curiosity as to whose spirit it may be.

Could it have been Esmerelda?

That encounter took place in the downstairs bedroom, though. Esmerelda's spirit was believed to inhabit an upstairs chamber–the Pink Room.

So, a little later, Eileen took it upon herself to find the woman who had been occupying the Pink Room and inquire–discreetly somehow–if she, in that room, had any feelings, any sightings.

A nervous Eileen was taken by surprise once again as the old woman answered in the affirmative.

Yes, from almost the very time she settled into the Pink Room, a gentle, almost comforting entity seemed to share her space there.

The woman described her invisible roommate as shy, happy, and quite restless.

The season passed, Eileen had a few tentative contacts with what she could have described as psychic energy, but never once did she claim to see or even sense the ghost of Esmerelda.

These days, it seems that neither guests nor innkeepers nor housekeepers feel ill at ease with the knowledge that there is a ghost at 22 Jackson.

The stories continue to be told and the energy continues to be felt and sensed. Esmerelda has made herself quite at home in the beautiful bed & breakfast inn.

Oh, there may be the occasional snit from Minerva, but generally, Esmerelda is just another special guest there.

But, as housekeeper Debbie Nordabi said, "It's too bad Esmerelda's not a cleaning ghost—we could always use a hand around here!"

What may we take into the vast Forever?
That marble door
Admits no fruit of all our long endeavor,
No fame-wreathed crown we wore,
No garnered lore.

...Edward Rowland Sill

The turret of The Inn at 22 Jackson Street

THE JERSEY DEVIL?

In the Wildwood Historical Society Museum, we came across
this passage in an ancient account of the "Jersey Devil":

*Upon such occasions Leed's Devil is seen in companionship of a beautiful golden-haired
woman in white, or yet of some fierce-eyed, cutlass-bearing disembodied spirit of a
buccaneer whose galleon, centuries ago,
was wrecked upon the shore of Cape May County."*

Whether or not the beast's companion is a ghost from a Cape May beach, the Devil itself
has been memorialized in the eclectic collection of curiosities at Menz Restaurant, Route
47, Rio Grande. Behind the counter, near one of the four two-headed calves on display,
is this depiction of the Jersey Devil, who some say may still roam the woods of Cape May
County. The "Devil" here was made by a Menz customer, and is, as the restaurant says,
"...a composite animal born of generations worth of hysterical descriptions."

Hey, I'm Here!

It took some time for Christie Igoe to become comfortable with the spirit that haunts her Sea Holly Inn.

She still seems to fill some of the more nervous gaps in conversations about her resident ghost with solicitous laughter.

There is no denying it, though, her charming little B&B at 815 Stockton Avenue is haunted.

"It's not something I really ever wanted to advertise," she said. But, recent publicity in several media has called attention to the benign but busy entity. It hasn't seemed to hurt business one bit.

Christie's own charm and the hospitality of the beautiful gingerbread inn more than make up for any stray sounds and sightings guests may discover there.

What is now the Sea Holly was once a private residence and later a boarding house. It is said that actresses and actors used to frequent the place, and that it was the site of certain romantic intrigue from time to time.

There is some speculation that the ghost which has made itself quite evident in the inn is that of a maid who carried on an affair in the early years of the building's existence.

While nobody knows for certain just who the spirit may be, Christie and others are quite sure that it has no qualms about manifesting itself.

"It all started the first year we bought the place," Christie said. "When we were doing restorations I would hear a lot of things. I would hear footsteps.

"At one point, I went upstairs all the way to the third floor thinking someone had come into the house through the fire escape. Of course, nobody was there."

Her demeanor changed after some of that aforementioned nervous laughter. Christie recalled the times her late husband, Christopher, also experienced the phantom sounds.

"My husband was alive at the time and I would tell him about it. I'd say that I'd swear there was something in the house. Well, he thought I was nuts.

"But when he would be down here helping me with the interior work, he would start to hear the footsteps. And then, within the next couple of months after that, he started seeing a shadowy figure in one of the windows in the back.

"We were very sure that there was something here. So, we talked to someone who was into ghosts and asked if they knew anyone who could read a house.

"They did, so we got in touch with her."

The psychic asked to, and received permission to, spend some nights in the Sea Holly.

"She had experiences," Christie reported.

Unsettling events unfolded as the psychic encountered the presence. Once, her bed shook noticeably. Another time, she felt that same bed sag as if someone–or something–else was sitting on one end.

Christie said the psychic told her that in all her

investigations of haunted places, it was one of the most intense experiences she had ever had.

The energy seemed to be strongest on the third floor, which was once the servants' quarters in the building's early years as a private home.

The psychic felt the spirit was undoubtedly female, and likely that of a servant. A high level of spirit activity was also noticed on a back staircase which was once used exclusively by servants.

Christie Igoe said some of her suspicions were borne out by the psychic's readings.

"I also have seen a shadowy figure in that hallway back by the kitchen," she confirmed.

"Every once in a while there are things moved in there. A plant will be in a different place, and things like that.

"It all happens when nobody's here, so I know it's not just somebody moving things around. No one else is around."

Christie recalled one startling incident.

"I was in the kitchen once and I had an old hutch in the kitchen. There was an old key in the glass door of the hutch.

"One day, all of a sudden, that key came flying just over my head!"

As a warship fires a shot across the bow of another vessel as a firm warning, the "flying key" episode may have been the sign Christie was waiting for.

"It was like 'Hey! I'm here!'

"It didn't hit me or anything. It was far above my

Shadowy figures have been spotted in the Sea Holly Inn on Stockton Avenue.

head. Somebody was trying to let me know they were around. So, we just started accepting that fact," Christie said through, well, nervous laughter.

As we humans must codify, identify, animate, and illustrate that which we cannot understand, Christie named her friendly but demonstrative housemate. She named her Elizabeth.

"I called her Elizabeth, only because it was the first name that came to mind," she laughed (nervously).

Whatever its actual name might have been, and whoever it may have been in life, the ghost of the Sea Holly has provided some literal chills and figurative thrills for those who work and stay at the inn.

"It's mostly when the house is empty and really quiet when I hear it," Christie continued. "Of course, it's more obvious because no one else is around.

"I have had guests in one particular room on the third floor who have come down and have no idea there's anything about a ghost here.

"But they came down and asked if there was something going on in that room, because their bed shook that night.

"I once had a woman who was in that room. She said she felt a cold chill go through her body," she added.

"What's amazing," she concluded, "is that it's not necessarily or even usually people who want there to be a ghost up there. Nine times out of ten when they ask me something, they have no idea that there really is something here."

Christie has permitted two seances at her inn, and is

growing more and more comfortable with the notion that she shares her beloved inn with a shadowy form that likes to play tricks with those who drop by.

"I'd like to think the ghost is a kind woman waiting for someone, or for something to happen.

"Maybe it's a sad ghost, looking out to sea in hopes her man would soon come back to her," she mused, her nerves fading into romantic rumination.

A PHANTOM IN THE PHYSICK MANSION?

When the Mid-Atlantic Center for the Arts (MAC)was established in 1970, its goal was, among other things, to purchase and renovate the 18-room, 1879 home of Dr. Emlen Physick.

The mansion was designed by the noted architect Frank Furness, and is recognized as one of the finest examples of Victorian "Stick Style" architecture. Noting the deteriorating condition of the home and nine outbuildings on the four-acre estate, concerned citizens rallied to raise the money to establish what is Cape May's only museum of Victorian living.

It is ironic (or is it?) that MAC's first fund raiser was a Halloween party in the "haunted" Physick House. More than a million dollars and probably that many volunteer hours later, the mansion stands as a tribute to community concern.

That first event at the Physick House may have been more than happenstance.

It is believed that one room (left) of the mansion holds within it the ghost of a former resident.

Dr. Physick, grandson of Dr. Philip Syng Physick, considered to be the "Father of American Surgery"; and great-great-grandson of Philip Syng Jr., the silversmith who created the inkwell used by the signers of the Declaration of Independence, was himself a champion of Cape May and before his death in 1916 was quite active in civic affairs.

He never married, and lived in the house with his maiden aunt Emilie and widowed mother, known in history as Mrs. Ralston.

It is the ghost of this "Mrs. Ralston" which even the most staunch non-believers and stoical cynics admit may very well remain in the Physick Estate.

Joanne Galloway, communications director at MAC, described the ghost as "Very happy." "She's pleased with what goes on in the house," Ms. Galloway continued, "and she likes that people are coming in."

While MAC remains somewhat aloof, *officially*, about its resident ghost ("I just want to make sure that people, when they come into the house," Ms. Galloway said, "don't think they'll be seeing things flying around!"), some of its tour guides will readily spin the yarns of their own encounters with the phantoms of the Physick Estate.

They might even have heard about the time a wheelchair (below) chased one of them out of Mrs. Ralston's room!

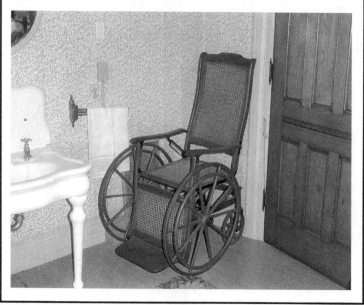

Some folks who work at the Winterwood shop on the Washington Street Mall believe a ghost inhabits the building. Prior tenants have also reported strange happenings there.

The Playful Poltergeist

To fully appreciate the story you are about to read, it is necessary to revisit a tale from our first volume of *Cape May Ghost Stories.*

In that book, we visited Keltie's book store at Washington Street and Draper Walk.

It was there that several individuals had experienced several entities over the course of several years.

Once a dentist's office, the 518 Washington Street building was haunted for a spell by that dentist.

A mysterious, translucent figure dressed in white was seen gliding through the first and second floors of the building. Accompanying the ghostly form as it passed by shocked witnesses was a soft breeze.

The distinct sound of young girls giggling could be heard as if in the distance—of time or place.

Books slipped out of shelves. Papers shuffled. Disembodied footsteps echoed through the store and upstairs living quarters.

Keltie's, almost anyone who lived or worked there agreed, was haunted.

What was the little book store is now the downtown Cape May location of the legendary Winterwood Gift and Christmas Shoppe.

Those who read what has turned out to be "Book One" of these tales of Cape ghosts will recall "Hester," the resident wraith of the original Winterwood in Rio Grande.

That thumping, rumbling, grumbling, and cherry tobacco-chewing ghost has pestered employees in the handsome Route 9 shop.

But it is not Hester, nor the old dentist we discovered on a return visit to the Keltie's corner. What plagues the people there now is a playful poltergeist.

Those who have been pestered by that poltergeist have—as those who have been pestered by the unknown often do—given their ghost an arbitrary name.

They call him Charlie.

Franke MacDonald was quite prepared when we came to call at Winterwood on the Washington Street Mall. She had prepared a four-page summary of the inexplicable occurrences which have disrupted the normal flow of activity at the busy shop where it's always the Christmas season.

"We have no idea what's going on here," she admitted. "Maybe the spirits became upset when we 'condoed' the building."

The structure was split into two retail spaces. Winterwood shares the building with another store. Although odd and perhaps ghostly things have reportedly happened in the "other side" of the building, the operators of the shop declined to comment.

Ms. MacDonald had no problems with whatever she and her fellow workers at Winterwood have encountered.

"Most of the things happen between 10 and 11 at night," she said.

"One of the most interesting things took place during the very first year we moved in after Keltie's [book store] moved out.

"Everything in the rooms appeared to be quite empty, but way in the back corner I got up on a ladder and there was one book that was left behind when Keltie's left.

"That one book was a book on parapsychology!"

With that rather ominous discovery and perhaps obvious "sign," the conversion from book store to Christmas gift and decoration shop proceeded.

And, it wasn't long until the ghosts came to call.

"We figure he's either an adolescent ghost or a dirty old man ghost," Franke says of Charlie.

She bases that statement on the fact that most of the strange things which have happened there have happened to the primarily young and primarily female staff.

Take a ghost which could be either a young prankster or a cranky oldster, add four or five young women, and the stories can become quite convoluted.

"Our spirit likes to tease the young sales girls," Franke continued.

"One would go downstairs for a box for a customer's purchase and come up empty-handed in the stock room. The next girl would go downstairs and confirm that the item was nowhere to be found.

"The third girl would go down there and within seconds find the item in plain sight, sometimes in the middle of the floor where it really shouldn't have been!

"One girl, Heather, went down to the stock room to get a Barber Shop Christmas village figure for a customer

CAPE MAY GHOST STORIES · BOOK TWO

who wanted one.

"She couldn't find any Barber Shops, but noticed a Tailor Shop in stock.

"She went back upstairs and told the customer that we didn't have a Barber Shop, but had a Tailor Shop. The customer said he'd take the Tailor Shop.

"So, Heather went back down to get the Tailor Shop. It wasn't there. The Barber Shop was, though.

"She was happy, because the customer had originally wanted the Barber Shop. So, she brought the Barber Shop up instead. The customer was also happy, and said they'd take *both* buildings.

"Heather went back down to get the Tailor Shop, which hadn't been there the last time she was down. But this time, there it was, in the middle of the floor!"

Ms. MacDonald claims that Charlie can be helpful, too.

"On a particularly busy Saturday evening I went in search of a box. Rushed and frustrated, I muttered 'Come on, Charlie—enough's enough, where's the box?'

"Then, the strangest thing happened. From within a styrofoam-packed, unopened box, a music box began to play the song, 'Toyland.'

"I turned around, totally confused and surprised, and there was the box I had been looking for, right in front of me."

Most folks who have worked at Winterwood on Washington Street have had some kind of quirky contact with Charlie.

"When we were upstairs, we all would hear footsteps

66

on the steps leading to the stock room. Then, when we were downstairs, we would hear footsteps overhead in the store, which was empty at the time," she reported.

On one very busy night, the compact disc player jammed on the same disc for two hours.

The young staff was forced to listen to Frank Sinatra crooning "I'll Be Home For Christmas" until one of them was able to break free and change the CD.

"Just as Betsy put her hand on the door knob of the stock room," Franke said, "the CD automatically changed, and the player played on the random mode the rest of the night."

Franke MacDonald recalled the incident most recent from the time this book was researched.

"It was a Saturday evening before Halloween. Many of our customers were coming in after the Ghost Tour and asked about our ghosts.

"A young couple wanted an ornament personalized, and I ran the sale. I stepped back for the drawer to open, and as I did, a buzzer sound went off and a few seconds of random letters and numbers popped up on the register display.

"Another clerk asked what happened, since I wasn't anywhere near the register when all this happened. I jokingly replied, 'Charlie's just having fun.'

"The young couple gave each other a strange glance but said nothing. I laughed, gave them their change and asked what name they wanted on the ornament.

"The name they wanted was....Charlie!"

CAPE MAY GHOST STORIES · BOOK TWO

Reports of ghostly activities at the Craig House include one entity which may have made its presence known in a most unusual fashion.

68

The Sewing Ghost

In 1891, John F. Craig bought a handsome home at 609 Columbia Avenue at a sheriff's sale for the grand total of $7,500.

If he could see it now!

Craig's summer home, which was built just after the Civil War, stayed in his family until two of his six children, Susan and Martha, sold it to "outsiders" in the 1950s.

The building served as an apartment house until the bed & breakfast rebirth of Cape May in the 1980s when it became an inn.

In February, 1993, Frank and Connie Felicetti opened it as a delightful, restored Victorian B&B.

It is noteworthy for its wrap-around porch, two enclosed sun porches—one in which guests may enjoy the morning sun, the other in which the afternoon sun shines—a library with shelves of vintage volumes, and floor-to-ceiling doors which open to fresh breezes from the sea.

The Felicetti's introduction to what may be a permanent ghost, er, *guest*, came early on in their ownership of The John F. Craig House.

Their very first guests were four women—a mother, her two adult daughters and a grown granddaughter. They checked in to the Craig House for a weekend.

"It was the older woman who came down to us first,"

Connie recalled. "She was staying in Room 5, the Lucy Johnson Room, which we had named after the Craig family cook.

"It was one of the rooms used by servants in the oldest part of the house.

"She came down and thanked me for sewing a button on her slacks. Well, I said 'excuse me, but I'm not sure I know what you're talking about! I didn't sew a button on your slacks.'

"She said that she had left a needle and thread and button there, but hadn't gotten around to putting it on. When she went into the room that afternoon, the button had been sewed on."

Connie didn't sew it on. No one else in the Craig House staff did. The others in the woman's party said they didn't, either.

"We decided then," Connie said with a cautious chuckle, "that it must have been Lucy Johnson who did it."

During that first year of operation, the Felicettis were asked several times about the presence of any supernatural activity within the walls of their inn.

One particular woman, a friend of Connie's, stayed in Room 5, the "Lucy Johnson Room," and casually asked Connie if there were any ghosts floating around the place.

Connie told her of the button incident and other idle talk about spirits there.

"The woman looked at me very seriously," Connie said, "and told me that she had definitely felt a presence up in Room 5."

Another time, a young couple was packing their

luggage into the trunk of their car, preparing to leave after a quiet stay at the Craig House.

The woman approached Connie with what was now a somewhat familiar question. Were there any ghosts in the Craig House?

"I told her about Lucy," Connie recalled. "And she started jumping up and down on the driveway. 'I KNEW IT! I KNEW IT! I KNEW IT!' she said.

"Her husband put his hand up to his head and said she hasn't stopped talking about this all weekend.

"She said her husband didn't want her to ask me," Connie continued, "but she just had to because she sensed many things and knew there was spirit energy in the house.

"Among other things, one of the most obvious incidents in the night was when a closet door in the Lucy Johnson Room opened on its own."

While Room 5, the Lucy Johnson Room, seems to be the epicenter of the ethereal activity in the Craig House, some less tangible tales have come from guests who have stayed across the hall in Room 4, the Susan Craig Room.

"There was a young woman who came down and told us that she had intended to put a bottle of medicine on an air conditioner to keep it cool overnight.

"She went to bed, and in the middle of the night a dish of potpourri on her night stand fell to the floor. It made enough noise to awaken her.

"The dish hadn't been near the edge of the table or anything. It had to do a lot of moving to fall over the side.

"Anyway," Connie said, "it woke her up, and when it did, she noticed she had forgotten to place her medicine on

The Lucy Johnson Room is the site of the strongest energy in the Craig House.

the air conditioner."

The woman was seriously convinced that the dish falling for no apparent reason was a sign from something or someone in that room—something or someone who had been looking out for her.

Also in the Susan Craig Room is the strange story of a woman who was sleeping there, was awakened in the night, and saw a little, red-headed girl standing at the end of her bed.

The woman who had that experience is long gone from the Craig House, and could not be found.

But her story—her tantalizing little story about the ghostly red-headed lass in Room 4—remains indelibly etched in the annals of the John F. Craig House.

From ghoulies and ghosties
and long-leggity beasties…
And things
that go bump
in the night,
Good Lord,
deliver us!

…Scottish prayer

Jackson Street epitomizes Cape May's worldly (and, perhaps otherworldly) charm.

Jackson Street Jitters

Beads of moisture clouded the globe of the streetlight lantern.

A predawn rain dampened the sidewalks as the morning sun squeezed between the clouds.

The street glistened and the pastels of the inns along Jackson Street sparkled as a new day began in Cape May.

Peggy had walked this way, at this time, many times before.

She lives in West Cape May and works along Beach Drive.

"Many times," Peggy related, "I hoof it to work just around dawn. It's a wonderful walk. I can either cut through Congress or Perry or Jackson, and any of those ways is beautiful."

In return for her story, we promised to not use Peggy's real name or place of employment. "I'm afraid some people would call me a kook," she laughed. "And although those I work with already think I am a little loony, I think my boss would not be very happy if you revealed where I work. He's not exactly a believer in ghosts. Not at all."

Actually, Peggy wasn't much of a believer in ghosts—until one came to call on a crisp September morning on Jackson Street.

"The first thing I ever read about ghosts," she

continued, "was your first book about the ghosts here on the Cape. It looked interesting because it was about ghosts around where I live.

"When I first bought the book, I thought it was just a bunch of stories you had made up. I didn't realize it was about supposedly true stories in real places.

"Well, once I realized that, the whole notion took on a different meaning to me.

"I mean, could all these stories be made up by all those people? Could everyone—and I know some of the people who you interviewed—be lying about these things? I don't think so."

Peggy said she read the first *Cape May Ghost Stories* book, put it in a bookshelf, and never gave it much more thought.

"That was somewhere around 1988, I guess," she recalled. It was right when the book first came out.

"And, it wasn't until 1996 when I had my experience."

Peggy's "experience" is one of the most remarkable of any ever recorded by the team of ghost story hunters which has published more than 20 books on the subject.

"I will never understand what I saw that morning," Peggy sighed. "All I know is that I will swear in any court or church or synagogue that what I saw is what I saw, and it was all very real."

The fact that Peggy asked for anonymity not only shields her from ridicule, but it also sends a signal to the researcher and writer that she is not fabricating a story to gain publicity or notoriety for herself.

In the ghost-hunting, or more properly ghost *story-* hunting trade, one must become a fair judge of human character.

There are those who want every "i" dotted and every "t" crossed in their names—so their friends will be impressed that their name, and their presumably authentic story, made it to print in an actual book.

There are those whose spirits seem to rise not from the "great beyond" but more like a bottle or a flashback from the psychedelic '60s.

And there are those whose lips quiver and hands tremble as they carefully measure their words and their thoughts to recall and reveal most unsettling and unexplainable encounters with the unknown.

Peggy is of the latter characterization.

"It was just after five in the morning when I came out of my house to head to work.

"I headed down West Perry and turned down Jackson.

"I was yawning, I guess, and sipping on the cup of coffee I had in an insulated mug. I passed the bandstand and Washington Street, and headed toward work up on Beach.

"I got just past Carpenter's Lane when a car came past me. I thought to myself that it was unusually quiet that morning on the street. I mean, there's usually not a whole lot going on here at that hour, but that particular morning seemed deathly quiet.

"It all seems weird talking about it now, but I swear that it's just as I remember. I have to tell you that after that car went by, I was distracted to look up from my coffee and onto the street scene.

"I distinctly remember that I did a double take when it seemed to me that every leaf on every branch of every tree was totally still. It's like there was no breeze at all.

"OK, I thought then—and now—that was a little strange. Again, you'll have to remember that at the time I thought nothing about ghosts. Absolutely nothing.

"Well, that is, until I looked straight ahead, down Jackson Street, and noticed a woman walking on the other side of the street, what would be the northern side of the street.

"Of course, I didn't think anything was particularly odd, other than it seemed as if she didn't have any kind of jacket or even a sweater on, and it was definitely a jacket or sweater kind of morning.

"As I looked back and thought about it, I can't really remember at all what she was wearing. She appeared like out of nowhere and was pretty far away.

"Anyway, I was distracted for a second, and when I looked over to see the woman, she was gone.

"So, I figured she just popped into one of the places on that side of the street. I mean, I didn't give it any thought at all. It was no big deal at the time.

"That's what I thought until I remembered how quiet and eerie it had gotten. I gathered my thoughts and slowed down my walk. It was really, really strange. Again, no birds chirping, no sounds from other streets, it was as if time was standing still.

"I know this all sounds crazy to you, but it is the feeling I had that morning, and I will never forget it."

Peggy poured another cup of coffee as I flipped the

cassette tape over for the rest of her story. It is a story which may have you looking over your shoulders the next time you walk down Jackson Street.

This is not to infer that Jackson Street is a boulevard of the bizarre. It is one of the archetypal streets of Cape May–its first real street.

Known in the 18th century as "Cape Island Road," it was traversed by steamboat passengers and cargo connecting from the sea to the bay.

The first hotel in the little village of "Cape Island" was built on what is now Jackson Street in what is now Cape May in 1791.

In 1878, the fire which swept through more than 30 acres of the town consumed most of the buildings on Jackson Street. Within months after the debris was cleared, however, a "new" Jackson Street–with its familiar Edwardian and Victorian structures, was rebuilt.

Most certainly, there are tales to be told along Jackson Street. We'll now rejoin Peggy's tale.

"As I stood there, thinking about that woman and marveling at the silence, I heard a woman's voice coming from somewhere.

" 'Audrey,' it said. 'Audrey.'

"It was certainly a woman's voice, a young woman's voice. It seemed to come from the middle of the street. I know that sounds whacko, too, but it really did.

"And, because everything was so still during those few moments, it seemed to have an echo to it or something. I really can't explain it well.

"By that time, I started to think something was up. I

only had one cup of coffee, so it wasn't a caffeine buzz. All I know is that I heard the young woman calling out the name 'Audrey.'

"As I looked around to see where the sound was coming from, I slowed down to a stop and slowly turned my head from side to side.

"That's when I saw that same woman again!

"I thought, dammit, I was sort of scanning the whole street, and this lady came from out of nowhere. That's the first split second I thought I might be dealing with something like a ghost.

"Don't forget, I was not a believer in this stuff. Until, I guess, that moment.

"Again I heard the voice calling for 'Audrey.' And as I looked around, I glanced to the woman across the street. She seemed to stop and whirl around slowly. It wasn't as if she turned her head or anything, her whole body seemed to turn around.

"Then, I noticed that she really didn't have any real distinguishable features. It was fairly light enough for me to have noticed any facial features or clothing. But she seemed to be just a form, a figure.

"As I stared at her for what was probably five seconds, she actually seemed to just float, maybe an inch or two over the sidewalk.

"I'll tell you, by that time, I was getting a little scared. And yet, I didn't fear for my life or anything. I just wondered exactly what it was that I was seeing.

"I felt like I was suspended in some time warp or something. And then, the absolutely weirdest thing happened. All of a sudden, out of nowhere, an icy chill—I know, the kind I heard about in other ghost stories, the kind I didn't believe could ever really happen—just seemed to brush past me. It was very, shall I say, chilling—in more ways than one.

"I remember that I sort of scrunched up my shoulders when the coldness swept through me.

"Almost immediately, I looked around me. The woman had vanished once again. And, you know what? I started to hear things again. Birds, a car, the distant ocean surf. It was like everything had come back to life.

"It was warmer, lighter, louder, and much more comfortable.

"There was no lady across the street, nobody whispering 'Audrey,' and no deathly silence.

"I kind of brushed it all off mentally, took another sip of coffee, and kept walking down Jackson Street to work.

"As I approached Beach, some guy was coming around the corner onto Jackson. He said 'good morning' to me. I wished him a good morning, too. If he only knew!

"I got to work a few minutes later, and one of my co-workers came in and said, "Hey, Peggy, how's it going so far this morning?'

"I kind of chuckled and said, 'same old stuff.'

"If I had been truthful about how it was going so far that morning, she would have thought I was nuts.

"I guess I'll never know what went on that morning. Who that woman was, who 'Audrey' was—I guess I'll never find out.

"Maybe I don't want to!"

Her interview for this book was the first time Peggy revealed details of that morning on Jackson Street. She has told no one, not even close relatives, about it.

After that disconcerting episode, did Peggy ever again walk down Jackson Street to work?

"The very next morning," she laughed. "Like that guy said in the song, 'I ain't afraid of no ghosts.'"

"At least," she concluded, "until one chases me!"

Peter? Is That You?

The Peter Shields Inn employs a wonderful phrase to sell its seaside location to prospective guests.

"At the Peter Shields Inn," the brochure touts, "the ocean is your closest neighbor."

At 1301 Beach Drive, the tall columns and regal portico of the Georgian masterpiece fronts the beach and sea, and presents a stunning welcome to all who come to dine or relax in one of the seven ocean-view guests rooms.

The inn is in many ways reminiscent of the grand mansions of Newport. And, with a little research into just how the inn got to look as it does and be located where it is, there are some parallels between the old summertime playground of the wealthy in Rhode Island and the genteel resort town of Cape May.

Peter Shields' mansion was built 20 years after the fire which raged through downtown Cape May. As the businesses and hotels there rebuilt, there were those in "East Cape May" who believed the resort towns there could become the Newport of the Garden State.

Peter Shields was head of the Cape May Real Estate Co., and had a vision of a grand hotel on the oceanfront—an anchor for what would surely be a building boom along the largely undeveloped area around Sewell Point.

Concurrent with the construction of Shields' stately

Several employees have witnessed ghostly goings-on in the restaurant of the Peter Shields Inn.

mansion, the Philadelphian also supervised the construction of that "grand hotel."

The mansion was completed in 1907. One year and one million dollars later, the Hotel Cape May opened as the largest (and, it was said, world's first fireproof) hotel on the Cape.

For all it was, and it indeed was spectacular, the thoroughly modern hotel never quite lived up to its expectations. Ditto for the "Newport of the Garden State."

The Hotel Cape May was requisitioned as a military hospital during the first World War, and later was the Christian Admiral Hotel.

The building was demolished in 1995.

As the fortunes of the Cape May Real Estate Co. fell, so fell the fortunes of Peter Shields and, in a sense, his mansion.

The home lapsed into periods of use as the home of the Cape May Tuna Club, a temple of transcendental meditation, a "gentleman's gambling club," and a brothel.

In 1989, the popular and talented chef Ron Panczner became owner and chef of the Peter Shields Inn's restaurant. The Culinary Institute of America graduate had paid his dues over more than a decade of experience in other fine restaurants in and near Cape May.

Chef Panczner readily admits that his restaurant, which sprawls over the first floor of the inn, may hold within a ghost.

A harmless, aimless ghost, perhaps. But a ghost just the same.

The story of *who* haunts the restaurant and how

whomever it may be met their demise becomes somewhat skewed.

Legend has it, though, that the energy of one member of the Shields family—who could have drowned in the surf in front of the mansion or could have been killed in a hunting accident near Two Mile Beach—remains within the walls of the structure.

"The family packed up and left here somewhere around 1912," said Ron Panczner. "But he's been visiting us ever since!"

The "he," many people believe, is none other than Peter Shields himself.

The restaurant's manager concurs with Chef Ron, and told us of one incident that proved a bit unnerving to all involved.

"A grandson of Peter Shields was here," the manager said, "and when he stayed here all the lights kept going out. He ate in three different dining rooms during his stay, and wherever he was, the lights went off!"

Ron Panczner has a theory about the spunky spook. "Apparently, he likes the ladies. He hangs around them a lot.

"Our waitresses have often sighted him in the hallway down by the ladies' room. In the ladies' room the lights have flickered on and off for some of the girls.

"It's always been generally calm and harmless," he concluded.

One waitress, who wished to remain anonymous, related her encounter.

"I was walking down the hall in the basement and I just felt something on my shoulder. And, a weird sound or something happened. It was just a split second."

Another waitress who also asked to remain nameless, said she actually saw an apparition in that lower hallway.

"I can't say I saw a ghost," she said, "but I guess there's no other explanation.

"I was walking to the ladies room after the customers had cleared out, and I saw all I can describe as a milky-white form kind of slithering down the hall about six or seven feet in front of me.

"It almost looked like it was clinging to the one wall. It happened quickly, and I didn't see it very long. But it was definitely there, and it was definitely strange.

"I didn't know that others had felt that the place had a ghost in it until after my experience. I still don't believe in ghosts, but I believe in what I saw that time."

"So," she sighed, "maybe ghosts do exist. But it'll take a lot more than that to prove it to me."

Karen Paxton, who worked in the Peter Shields kitchen at the time of this writing, had a similar experience.

"At the end of the night I was walking along that hallway that goes to the rest rooms and I looked over my shoulder and saw that two of my coworkers were following me.

"I turned around and they were gone! I went back up and asked them if they had been downstairs and they said no.

"I definitely saw someone behind me, but no real person was there," she said.

Another employee, Barry Deckenbach, remembered the time he encountered something very odd in the downstairs area of the old mansion.

"I came in one morning very early and went into the dry storage area and I saw, of all things, a rattle.

"I never saw it before. I thought it was something that fell off a shelf. I turned around and there was a slight cloud or something in the room. No sooner did I see it, it disappeared."

A long-time resident of Cape May ("don't use my name or they'll think I'm a whacko!") told us she has heard many stories about the ghost in Peter Shields.

"It's totally benign," she told us in confidence. "And I don't think it has anything to do with Peter Shields himself. If that's what some folks choose to believe, well so be it. I think it's something far removed from Peter Shields or even his era.

"I think it may be something to do with the Indians, or maybe even a shipwreck or pirates," she claimed.

Whatever caused whomever from wherever to linger, the Peter Shields Inn ghost has quietly drawn much attention. At least one elementary school class in town has "adopted" the ghost and has gone in search of it.

Ron Panczner confirmed that psychics have visited his restaurant and have contributed their findings to the legend.

"As soon as they walk in the door," Chef Ron said of the psychics, "they say they can feel a very strong presence.

"As for me," the enlightened restaurateur added, "I've never seen anything. But I wouldn't say that it couldn't happen."

Several psychics have detected spirits in Room Two of the Thorn and the Rose Victorian apartments on Stockton Avenue.

Room Two

A steady rain pelted the hood of my jacket as I leaped over gutter puddles and onto the front porch of the Thorn and the Rose, 822 Stockton Ave.

I rang the doorbell, but the door was ajar, so I let myself in and offered a strong "hello!" to anyone in earshot.

The narrow foyer was dim and inviting. There was a warmth to the place, not only because it provided refuge from the wet and chilly Pearl Harbor Day afternoon, but for some inexplicable reason which at first escaped me.

A soft "hello" from the end of the hall answered me, and Laura Calnan emerged. Her red sweater shone in the darkness.

It was what research partner David Seibold and I call a "cold call." We had heard there was a ghost in the Thorn and the Rose, and we had come unannounced to speak with Laura, if she so desired.

Laura stood with her back to the staircase. We had called at an awkward time. We should have known better. It was check-in time at the inn. More important visitors were soon to arrive. No innkeeper in Cape May could, would, or should be expected to talk about that which glides by night when those who pay by day are about to come.

Still, Laura granted us what time she could until her guests arrived.

She stood with her back toward the staircase. As the conversation funneled from generalities and cordialities and into things ghostly, I found her native New England accent most charming and her mannerisms reassuring.

My attention was rooted to her every word, to be sure. But as she spoke, my eyes were distracted by the very obvious movement of someone–a housekeeper, a guest, someone–on the landing at the top of the stairs.

With no doubt whatsoever in my mind, a shadow–and then another shadow–crossed slowly from right to left up there.

The shadows, I reasoned, were cast by someone in a hallway which lay above where we were standing.

Unfazed, I hoped, by any darting of my eyes she may have detected, Laura told of the ghosts in her Victorian apartments and graciously asked if we would care to see the room which has had the most spirit activity reported.

Before we were to ascend the stairs, I asked, almost academically, if there was anyone upstairs.

Laura's shoulders dropped and her eyes widened as she nervously said no. There was no one upstairs.

Then what I saw–those shadows,–were cast onto the door at the top of the stairs by something from the *outside*. There was certainly an explanation.

Laura seemed genuinely interested in hearing more about my casual sighting. Slowly, we walked up the staircase and I repeated my story. The shadows were most definitely there, they most definitely moved, most definitely were cast upon the white bedroom door at the very top of the stairs, and most probably came from a source in the hall or through a front window.

When we reached the landing at the top of the stairs, Laura told me to look around. There were no windows whatsoever in the hallway. No windows through which shadows could be cast. No housekeeper. No guests.

As I pondered that fact, she told of the one room in her building which has been the site of the ghost reports.

It was the room beyond the white door upon which the mysterious shadows had been cast.

Room two.

There are stories to be told about that room. Many stories.

Laura and Brad Calnan purchased the apartment building in 1991, and had the Thorn and The Rose up and running by the Fourth of July weekend.

During the period of extensive renovations, odd things happened. Doors opened and closed on their own and untraceable sounds caught their attention, but Laura and Brad were too busy working to worry about any significance they might have had.

It wasn't long until they were introduced to what may have been attempting to introduce itself to *them*—the ghosts.

A self-described medium came to call over the Independence Day holiday. She and a male companion were passing through Cape May on their way to New York City. They sought and found accommodations at the Thorn and The Rose, in the only room open at the time.

Room two.

All was well as the guests checked in and settled into their charming room.

Just after midnight, though, Laura heard a banging on her door. It was the woman, frantically complaining that there was a ghost in the room.

"I said 'what? what?'," Laura remembered. "I didn't know I had a ghost!

"I asked the woman if she had seen this ghost, if she had talked to it or it had talked to her. She said 'yes.'

"I said 'what? what?'. Then, she insisted that I go upstairs with her. So I went up and went into the room. I got goosebumps. It was summertime, but it was cold up in that front room.

"Then, the woman said, 'don't you see her?'

"I didn't see a thing. The woman told me the ghost she detected was French. Or, at least she was speaking French.

"At that point, my eight-year old son came into the room. He asked if everything was OK. I told him there was nothing to be worried about.

"Then, all of a sudden, he started speaking in French! I thought he was dreaming or something. I was shocked!

"Well, my guest's companion came into the room and started speaking French–and my son started answering him!

"I just grabbed my son and asked what's going on here! What are you doing to my child? I took my boy back downstairs and I stayed with him for a while. He seemed all right. He went back to sleep.

"When he woke up, he couldn't remember a thing."

Laura said her guests had no prior contact with her son, which would largely rule out hypnotism or collusion.

"I was actually prepared to ask the guests to leave,

Room Two.

and when I went back upstairs to do so, they had lit candles and had started some sort of seance.

"The woman said there were three spirits present: A little child and two sisters. And, they were very distraught.

"The man started talking in French again. Then, he said one of the ghosts had been killed on the other side of the house by someone who had been very close to them. And, the ghost wanted to talk to *me*.

"I said no, no, I didn't want any part of it. So, I left, and the woman guest called a little later and told me everything was OK, and the ghosts would let them alone. She also told me the ghost had me confused with someone else."

Laura didn't know what to make of the bizarre exchange in the wee, small hours. She went to bed and figured she try to reason it all out in the morning.

The guests slipped out quietly, but left a note saying all was quiet the rest of their night. But, they felt it their obligation to inform Laura and Brad that there indeed was a ghost—three ghosts, in fact, in...

Room two.

Later that summer, without provocation or predisposition, more untoward events gave Laura pause and cause to believe there may very well be something supernatural going on in her beloved apartments.

"The sound was heard of what seemed to be a child bounding a ball—as if playing jacks," she continued. "It would only happen when the fire siren would go off at night. Any time the fire siren sounded, we or certain guests would hear the faint *boom...boom...boom*. We had, maybe, four people hear it.

"Other times, we'd hear what sounded like a squeaky wagon, or tricycle. We couldn't figure it out."

Laura started to keep a running journal of the events, all the while trying to figure out exactly what was happening, and why.

Soon enough, some of the questions were to be answered.

Laura's friend and across-the-street neighbor, Christy Igoe, had already gone through some of what Laura was now experiencing.

Christy's quaint Sea Holly Inn had its own ghosts (detailed in an earlier chapter of this book), and a respected psychic had arrived to "read" the Sea Holly.

As the woman got out of her car at the Sea Holly, she was drawn to a high level of energy she detected coming from across Stockton Avenue. From the Thorn and the Rose.

Intrigued by that energy, the psychic asked Laura if she could investigate her building, as well as the Sea Holly. Laura granted permission.

It didn't take long for the psychic to pinpoint the strongest energy in the Thorn and the Rose. It centered in one particular room.

Room two.

The psychic entered that room and Laura was stunned as she witnessed subtle but noticeable physical changes in the woman as she drew the energy from the room into her body.

As the woman divulged her findings regarding the room and the apartments, she generally reiterated and substantiated what the previous "reader" had told Laura.

There are multiple spirits in the Thorn and the Rose.

"She said that there were two female ghosts. The older of the two had a cane, and had trouble getting around. The other one was taking care of her."

The psychic's identification of a third entity shook Laura Calnan to the very deepest recesses of her comfort zone.

"The third ghost," Laura was told, "was a little boy...*pulling a wagon...and playing with a ball!*"

To be expected, Laura was astonished

But there was more.

The psychic went to the third floor and said that the wall which connects Laura's apartments with the adjacent property (vacant then and at this writing) was a veritable concourse for ghosts.

And, in a closer examination of the little boy's spirit, it was felt that the lad was, for whatever the reason, very afraid of fire.

Perhaps, it can speculated, *deathly* afraid?

That psychic returned later with a team of mediums and journalists, stayed at the Thorn and the Rose, and did further research which is yet to be released.

"And, about two weeks after they left," Laura recalled, "a Missouri family which had stayed with us in the past stayed on the second floor.

"After they had settled, their pregnant daughter came down to join me on the porch and very calmly and without prompting informed me that she had a very strong feeling that there was a ghostly presence in her room."

Room two.

The psychics who visited Laura's lovely accommodations suggested ways to deal with the ambient energy there–sprinkle sea salt around affected areas, hang wooden crosses, etc.

Laura performed these precautionary acts, and the ghosts have seemed to be soothed somewhat.

Never has a harmful or threatening event taken place between the real and unreal beings at the Thorn and the Rose.

And, closely analyzing all of it, what can be threatening about a little boy bouncing a ball? Or a little old lady with a cane?

"People will ask me if I'm scared," Laura concluded. "I tell them no, I have never felt threatened. I'm used to it."

It was Franklin D. Roosevelt who adapted an entry from the journal of Henry David Thoreau and in his first inaugural address in 1933 delivered a phrase that should be remembered and restated by those who seek and/or find ghosts.

Thoreau's words were, "Nothing is so much to be feared as fear."

"The only thing we have to fear," the late president later said, "is fear itself."

Of course, FDR never stayed in that one particular chamber of the Thorn and the Rose.

Room two.

Where entity and quiddity
The ghosts of defunct bodies, fly.

Samuel Butler

A former guest at the Hotel Macomber on Beach Avenue continues to pay visits to the popular Cape May inn.

The Visitor

Every year, she arrives. In the dark of night, in the light of day, she comes. She stays. She goes.

No one ever sees her. No one can describe her. But many have felt her presence.

The presence, they say, of the ghost of the Hotel Macomber.

Actually, make that the *ghosts* of the Hotel Macomber.

There are two spirits which wander within the walls of the Macomber—one which has never been seen and one which has made itself known to several individuals over the years.

It would stand to reason that a wayward wraith might enjoy returning to the Macomber. When built at the turn of the century, it was the last historic landmark building erected in Cape May and the largest frame structure east of the Mississippi River.

In 1992, Charles and Crystal Czworkowski purchased the sturdy shingle-style hotel and completely renovated into a comfortable oceanfront inn.

Its Union Park Dining Room and its chef have won several awards, and the hotel has had a steady stream of repeat guests since its rebirth.

One of those guests may be encountered in Room 10 of the Hotel Macomber.

Then again, she may not be.

CAPE MAY GHOST STORIES · BOOK TWO

What has been described through psychic readings as the ghost of an elderly woman held over from just before the turn of the century has been felt in that room

Never manifesting itself as a full apparition, the energy has nonetheless created anxious moments for those who work and stay in that third-floor room.

Lights turning themselves on and off, articles lost and then found, strange sensations and sounds–things like that have vexed visitors from time to time.

All who have been touched in some way by this invisible visitor agree it seems to be more mischievous than menacing.

One psychic who confirmed the spirit's presence to this writer believed the ghost is that of a woman who did not die in the room, or even the hotel.

She was a frequent guest, however, and during her many visits there became quite friendly with a child of a previous owner. It is that connection, the psychic claimed, that brings the gentle woman's spirit back to the Hotel Macomber time after time.

That independent finding dovetails with the Czworkowskis belief that the old woman of room ten seems to enjoy having children around her.

That attribute is true, they say, for the other ghost which roams through the restaurant.

Legend has it that the spirit is of a woman who worked in the kitchen of the hotel many years ago. She died in the pre-Heimlich Maneuver era after choking on food.

Part of what was her life force remains in that same kitchen, particularly in a large walk-in storage room.

Crystal's sister-in-law, Diana Czworkowski, has had direct contact with the kitchen ghost, as have several other workers there.

While a certain level of spirit activity remains constant at the Hotel Macomber, much of what led its owners to truly believe their place is haunted has settled down a bit since the major renovations were completed.

Still, the ghosts of room ten and the kitchen remain rambunctious enough to add a certain character to an already splendid old hotel.

There is a Reaper whose name is death,
And, with his sickle keen,
He reaps the bearded grain at a breath,
And the flowers that grow between.

...Henry Wadsworth Longfellow

The Squeaking Gate

We shall call them Jean and Dan. It's not their real names, and we've promised to not disclose address or name of their lovely Columbia Avenue bed & breakfast.

In return for that pledge, they in turn promised to tell the tale of their resident ghost.

They call the spirit of their B&B Catherine, and how that name came about is interesting. Keep reading.

When Jean was asked when and how they had the first inkling that something unseen may walk among them, she said it was in the early 1990s, when she and Dan purchased the place.

"For many years, the gate and the fence that's around our inn now was not there. But, I used to hear a noise that sounded just like a squeaking gate opening and closing," Jean said.

It was not from a neighboring property, not from another door, not from anything easily identifiable.

"I'd hear it every so often. I'd hear that squeaking gate opening and closing when there was no gate there."

That mystery aside, there were indications in the 1871-era building that a decidedly feminine spirit was ensconced there.

"When Dan's aunt was still alive," Jean continued, "she came to help out at the inn and said she would pick up the aroma of a perfume. I think she said she believed it was 'Chantilly.'

"She and others would also smell some kind of spice, I think it was cinnamon."

The aromas that wafted through the inn were pleasant, and seemed to signify the presence of a Victorian-vintage woman whose spirit was trapped within Jean and Dan's inn.

The couple once rented out the third floor front room, and Jean believes it is there the energy is the strongest. The last tenants to rent that room, a couple Jean called "Don" and "Diane," may have stirred up the spirit, which reciprocated in a frightening fashion.

"They told us that they were feeling as if someone was shaking their bed. This happened a couple of times. Then, finally," Jean said, "the ghost made herself known to Don.

"She communicated with him through psychic thoughts, and she told him her name was Catherine."

In that psychic message, the spirit was specific about the spelling of her name. Catherine. With a "C."

"She instructed Don to ask his wife who Herbert Hofnagel was," Jean recalled. "So, Don did, and to everyone's amazement, she told him it was the name of her brother's Boy Scout leader.

"Well, we figured there's got to be something there, because prior to that, Diane and Don never had any reason to, nor did, discuss her brother's Boy Scout leader!"

It was a name out of the blue, Jean said. Never once had Don heard the name, and Diane was miffed when he (at the ghost's psychic instruction) asked about Mr. Hofnagel.

Jean has some theories about Catherine. She suspects she was a servant, as her spirit has been detected most often in a room which was known to have been a servant's quarters when the inn was a private home.

"I thought maybe Catherine might have been jilted by a lover, and that's why her ghost remains in the house," she guessed.

The ghost is generally quite docile, but there were times when some folks were a bit put off by the notion of sharing space with a spook.

"We once had two girls staying up on the third floor," Jean continued, "and they said they were leaving at the end of their agreement and they weren't coming back because of the ghost."

While hesitant to fully publicize their "haunted" B&B, Jean and Dan are good-natured about it all. A while ago, Dan was rummaging through knickknacks at a sale and found a whimsical, white, ceramic ghost.

For a couple of bucks, he picked it up and placed it in the parlor to signify Catherine.

The most telling incident involving the gate-swinging, bed-shaking, perfume-wearing Catherine the ghost took place when the innkeepers were updating their brochure.

"We had a professional photographer come in," Jean explained.

"All I can say is that we captured an image. It looked like clouds, but it was definitely the form of a person.

"I had just seen a TV documentary on ghosts, and on that program I saw something that was very, very similar to what we captured on that photograph.

"The thing is, there were two poses, exactly alike. The one had the image on, the other one didn't, and they were taken within seconds of each other.

"I knew that when I saw that picture, it was the picture of a ghost.

"Maybe," Jean concluded, "it really was Catherine."

A ceramic ghost represents "Catherine" in the parlor of the Columbia Avenue bed and breakfast.

Afterword

Will there be a *Cape May Ghost Stories, Book 3*?
Probably not.
Could there be a *Cape May Ghost Stories, Book 3*?
Most definitely.

The reality is that during the pavement-pounding, the door-knocking, the phone-calling, and the e-mailing it took to compile this second book, there were many more fruitless queries than there were actual stories.

This, of course, is to be expected.

Chief researcher Dave Seibold and I are accustomed to chasing down false leads. We know all too well what it is like to spend hours with individuals whose stories seem blatantly fabricated, and come away with a non-story. Or, to suffer through a lengthy discourse from someone whose "ghosts" seem to rise not from the "other side," but from an episode of '60s flashback.

Worse yet, we know the feeling of being brushed aside as some sort of literary pariahs bent on poisoning the minds of anyone foolish enough to read our efforts.

We have had doors slammed in our faces more than we care to remember. But, it's all in the game.

During the winter of 1996-97, when most of the research for this book took place, we were given several tips on Cape May places where ghosts are said to dwell.

Many of those tips came from individuals who had first-hand knowledge of the hauntings, because they were the ones who experienced them.

While those persons were more than willing to share their stories, either they or we insisted that the owners of the affected properties be contacted and their permission to use the stories be obtained. That, too, is all in the game.

In one particularly frustrating case, we received a bona fide lead, even a full interview which could have been developed into a chilling, five-page story–but were stymied when the owner of the bed & breakfast in which the incident took place refused to allow her establishment to be mentioned.

For reasons known only to herself, the B&B owner did not feel it was her best interest to associate her inn with (gasp!) ghosts.

So, we folded our notebook closed, shared shrugs of frustration with the inn's manager, and went on our merry way to a more enlightened and cooperative innkeeper.

Yes, dear reader, there are more–many more–ghost stories to be told on the streets and in the inns of Cape May. Indeed, some of the best-known B&Bs and hotels in town harbor very interesting spirits.

You'll have to discover them on your own in discussions with a housekeeper or underling employee over dinner, on a porch, or in a common room.

Just make sure the owners don't hear you!

To be fair, there is an argument that the presence of a ghost, or even the rumor of one, could affect business at a B&B, hotel, or restaurant.

It has been our experience, however, that those who have approved their ghost stories or legends for publication almost invariably discover that the affect is positive.

Certainly, some prospective customers may shy away, or be frightened away from an establishment for fear of the spirits which may inhabit it.

But, most savvy hoteliers seem to believe that a forthright, honest ghost story or legend gives a place character.

Indeed, the fact that Cape May harbors so many intriguing ghost stories along its storied streets gives the entire town a sense of character.

On several occasions, we approached an owner of a B&B and asked if they had any reports of ghostly activity in their inn.

Searching their memory and finding none, they often looked around at the Edwardian, Victorian, or Georgian architecture; at the period furnishings; at the rich and warm decor of their pride and joy and quipped something like, "No, can't say as there are any ghosts here, sorry. But the place *looks* haunted, doesn't it?"

And that, dear reader, is the magic of this place called Cape May.

It *looks* haunted.

And, it is.

Charles J. Adams III
Cape May, N.J.   April, 1997

023579

ON LINE   DATE DUE c. 2

JAN 0 2 2003	

GAYLORD   PRINTED IN U.S.A.